INFERNO OF REDEMPTION

ALAINA T. LEE

CONTENT WARNING

- Body dismemberment
- Rape with a weapon
- Drugging
- Degradation
- Sex trafficking (in mention)
- Abortion (in mention)
- Past trauma
- Dark content
- Rape of a minor
- Murder
- Forced Cannibalism
- Sexual Assault
- Evisceration

FOREWORD

This book is an interconnected book, which means you do not need to read the first two books before this one; however, it is recommended. Reading the "Angel" Series will give you more insight to Giselle and Elias' family background. You may also read it after, if you are you wondering more about them.

ORDER OF THE ANGEL SERIES

Tantalized
Insatiable

BOTH BOOKS ARE AVAILABLE ON KU AND AMAZON, ENJOY!

For every woman out there, that thinks they aren't strong enough to fight their demons. Grab those fuckers by their throats and make them pay. Your voice is loud, your actions are louder. Use them both. And do it with no regrets.

1

GISELLE

I didn't mean to fall for two people. I didn't mean to give my heart to someone and then turn around and wish I could share it with his best friend, too. But here I am, in the middle of my boyfriend, Elias, and his best friend, Hogan. The music is so intoxicating—or maybe it's me—my hands are up, and I'm in pure bliss. My brother and his fiancée are staring at us, but for the first time, I can't make myself care. Did I mention that Elias' *sister* is now engaged to my *brother*? Yeah, let's complicate shit even more: our entire family is at our vacation home in Rome, celebrating my brother, Graham's birthday. Yet here I am, unashamed, grinding on two men in front of them. Elias isn't oblivious to the attraction between me and Hogan—he's the one who wanted us to test it out.

"You look so fucking good dancing between us. How are we going to keep this a secret if you can't keep your fucking hands off Hogan? Hmm?" Elias growls in my ear while my hands run down the front of Hogan's shirt. I burst out in laughter, throwing my head back. Elias takes the opportunity and runs his tongue up my neck. I quickly look around before pulling them both upstairs to my room.

"Impatient, tonight?" Hogan asks, pushing me against the

wall. He's the rough one, the one who takes no mercy on me, the one who doesn't care if it hurts. He tells me that if I want soft, if I want slow, that I should go to Elias. But when I want it to hurt, I should always come to him. We've only done *this*, the three of us together, twice; both times we were so drunk that when I woke up, I got dressed and sneaked out, not wanting to face them in the morning.

"I think Liza saw us, she kept staring and then she said something to my brother," I tell them, ducking under Hogan's arm. Elias untucks his shirt and starts taking it off before heading towards the bathroom.

"She didn't see anything, we were dancing. Everyone is drunk. It's fine," he says, waving me off. I sit on the bed and Hogan sits next to me, the thought of sex clearly vanishing from his mind when he sees my face.

"He's right." He pulls my hands into his lap. "There was nothing to see, it was just us dancing." He pushes a piece of my hair behind my ear, and then quickly puts space between us. "Go take a shower with Eli, I'll see you in the morning."

That's how he is. Unless its sexual, he doesn't touch me. He waits for permission from me and Elias. I like that he wants to include us both, but the affection part has become hard to swallow. I know I shouldn't want both of them, I know I'd be judged, but I think it's unfair how women can't have what men always have. Why can't I love two men? Why the fuck can't I be with two men? If they're ok with it, then why the fuck does society make a woman feel like a goddamn slut if she's with more than one person?

Polyamorous is a thing. A very common thing, actually. I know because I was desperate and looked it up. The only problem is my family doesn't need me to add another target to the list. My father, before he died, finally decided to admit to my brother that he had us both kidnapped, raped, and tortured when we were younger—all so he could get more money. He trafficked women and was a part of a drug cartel. Now, my brother thinks that he's doing this job of keeping me out of the loop while he cleans up our father's mess.

I can't stop my mind from venturing off deeper, from thinking about how dangerous it would be to put *another* love interest into my life. It's not the fact that I would be judged that would be dangerous, but it's because Hogan would be publicly added to the list of people that matter to me. That list isn't a good list to be on, when you're a Salando.

2

GISELLE

"This is insane. Did you read this shit?" I ask, nudging Elias awake. I think I upset him earlier with my reaction last night, but we didn't talk about it. Instead, he just showered, climbed into bed, and kissed me goodnight. He groans and rolls over, wrapping his arm around my waist before nuzzling into my stomach.

"Being that I just woke up and its 4:00 a.m.? No, I haven't. What is it, princess?"

"This woman died because they wouldn't give her the medical care she needed." I shove the phone in his face, and his eyebrows draw together as he reads the article about a woman who was fifteen weeks pregnant and suffered internal bleeding from a car accident. But some douche bag of a doctor refused to operate on her, because she would have needed an abortion to even stand a chance of survival. So, the stupid fuck let her die. He literally let her fucking die.

"So, he wouldn't give her the abortion? The abortion that would've allowed him to do the surgery that would've saved her life? What in the actual fuck did I just read?"

"It's happening everywhere, Eli. Everywhere. Women don't

stand a chance anymore, especially those who are pregnant. It's fucking unfair. Men get to do and have whatever the fuck they want. Women? Oh, we have to walk on eggshells for everything we do."

He leans up on his elbow and stares at me, pulling my hands into his.

"Princess...what is this really about?" My eyes fill with tears, and he swipes it away when one falls down my cheek. "Why are you crying? Did you know her?"

I shake my head. "No...but she was twenty-three, Eli. She was young and died because she didn't get the patient advocacy she deserved. What if that were me?"

"That would never be you, for two reasons. One, we have our own family doctor who is paid to do whatever the fuck we say. And two, if we ever ended up in that situation, I'd kill the asshole who thought they'd stand in my way of saving you. We can have another baby, but I can't have another you."

"I'm not so sure of that...I don't think I can um, have kids."

"Why do you think that?"

"I..."

I'm staring at the doctor and all of these tools in front of us. I'm twelve. This isn't supposed to be my life. I should be home right now, but instead, I'm here. Kidnapped and constantly raped by men. There's nothing I can do about it. I still fight, but I'm growing weaker. Every time they rape me, I have to go see "the doctor" to make sure I'm not pregnant. And every time he gets more pissed off with me, because I'm "letting them touch what's his". He's so angry this time, that he promised to make sure I never have the chance to get pregnant. I watch him sterilize the tools before the procedure. And you know what? I can't say I'm putting up a fight this time.

"Where'd you go there, princess? You zoned out on me for a second," Eli says, bringing me back to reality.

"Don't worry, I'm going to take care of you."

"I'm sorry, I must be tired."

"Answer my question, why do you think that you can't get pregnant?"

"You'll never have to worry about this again."

"Because I'm...not on birth control. We don't practice safe sex, and you come inside of me every fucking chance you get. Plenty of times have been during ovulation. None of those times have I ended up pregnant. I just don't think I can." I shrug my shoulders and continue scrolling on my phone, as if I didn't just drop a bomb on him at four in the morning, then answer it with an even bigger lie.

"Giselle, look at me..." He tosses the phone out of my hand and cusps my chin to face him. "When we want a baby, we'll focus on having one. There are plenty of options if an actual doctor with a *degree* tells you that you can't. But in the meantime, stop putting such negative thoughts in that pretty fucking head of yours."

I lean my forehead against his before nodding my head at his words. He plants a soft kiss on my mouth.

"We're going to make a doctor's appointment for when we get back." I shake my head in protest. I don't need a doctor to tell me what I already know. The chances of me having a baby are slim to none after...It doesn't matter. I've prepared myself for that already, I don't need to be reminded again.

"No."

"Giselle, we're making the appointment. If we can't have children when we're ready, I'd like to know. I'd also like to see the look on your face when he tells you how wrong you are."

You have no idea.

When my mouth opens, he gently presses his finger against it to stop the protest that's brewing.

"Fine..." I mumble, reluctantly agreeing. He kisses the tip of my nose and smirks at me, before giving me the praise that I didn't know I needed until him.

"Good girl."

3

T he bathroom is full of steam as Eli stands there with his head submerged under the shower head. The water is beating down on him as he runs his fingers through his hair. I step in behind him, wrapping my hands around his waist. He leans into my touch, and I kiss the back of his bicep—I try to, at least. I'm tall—well, 5'7—but compared to his, 6'3 it's nothing.

"You, ok?" I ask. He nods but doesn't look at me. I turn him towards me and his eyes find mine. "What's wrong?"

"You almost freaked when you thought they knew something last night. But what's there to know?"

"What do you mean, *what's there to know*? I'm sleeping with my boyfriend and his best friend. Society doesn't make that ok for women."

"So, you plan on us continuing to do this?" he asks, rinsing the soap out of his hair.

"Well, I don't want to be labeled a slut, so yes. No one can ever find out about it."

"I'm not talking about that; I'm saying, am I going to continue to share my girlfriend with my best friend?" I step back and tilt my head at him. I'm taken aback by his words, because this wasn't something that I asked of him in the first place.

"This was your idea..."

"I know it was, but that wasn't my question."

"I heard your fucking question, Elias. I didn't ask for this, we never had to start in the beginning. It just happened. Stopping won't be an issue, either." I turn for the shower door, but he grabs my hand.

"Don't walk away from me, Giselle. We need to figure this out." I yank my hand away.

"Don't make me feel like *I* asked you to share *me*. I've always only wanted *you*. You were the one who got so fucked up and drunk that you offered me up on a goddamn silver platter to your best friend. Then you liked it so much, that *you* did it again."

"You said you wanted to do it, as I remember correctly. It was you asking me if I thought he *fucked* as good as he talked. You two flirt all the time. I like seeing you taken care of. I enjoy telling him what to do and watching him do it. But I didn't expect him to start entangling other feelings past sex so quickly."

I frown as he cuts the water off. I grab a towel as he grabs his wrapping it around his waist.

"What do you mean, what else could it be?" He sighs and brushes against my shoulder as he walks into the bedroom.

"He's falling in love with you, and I don't know whether I hate myself for it or if I should pat myself on my back for finding a girl who makes us both so fucking happy."

I can't help it—I laugh, loudly, because he's lost his mind.

"You're insane. Hogan does not love me. He might love *fucking* me, but he does not *love* me. That's it, we're done here. He won't touch me again. I'm not letting you and your stupid fucking fantasies ruin our relationship."

"Fantasies?" he asks as he climbs into bed. I ignore him and dress in my silk shorts and tank. "You might as well keep that off, Giselle."

I glare at him, and he raises his eyebrow when I don't move to undress.

"No," I say, folding my arms, willing myself to stand my ground. He's not going to insinuate that I'm the reason his best friend has fucked me and then think I'm going to be ok with it a moment later.

"No?" he questions, before slowly walking towards me. "Take it off. Now."

"I don't think I will. Maybe I'll go ask Hogan to take it off for me, ya know, since I *wanted* him so badly." He's on me so fast that I don't have time to react. A squeal slips from my lips, and a moment later, I'm being thrown onto the bed. My eyes quickly shut, and when they pop back open, they're met with anger and frustration seeping from Elias. I don't understand where this is coming from. He's acting like sharing me was the worst thing he could have ever done.

"Giselle, don't," he warns, his hand sliding up my tank before he yanks it up my body. I hesitate for a moment before obliging and lifting my arms as he slips it off. "Don't talk about him right now. Just me."

His voice is raw and laced with confusion; but I don't know what he could possibly be confused about.

"It's always you, Eli. Always. But you enjoy us doing this, I enjoy us doing this, too. We need to figure out what this is. Why is it so hard for you admit how much you like it?" His hands are entangled in my hair as his lips crash against mine. The kiss is brutal as our teeth clash against each other. I moan into his mouth when he tucks my lip between his teeth and bites down.

"It's not hard for me to admit it, I just want to make sure

you are ok with this. That you know this is your decision, it's your body, it's your choice."

"Baby, I appreciate it. But being worshipped by two men is every girl's dream. I feel like I belong to both of you. If you want us to continue to try this and see where it goes; I'm happy with that. If you want him to watch during sex until we figure this out completely, I'm happy with that, too."

"Yeah?" he asks. I kiss his neck and nod.

"I need to feel you," he whispers against my mouth as he yanks my shorts off in one swift motion. I'm glad I didn't bother wearing panties to bed, I'm sure he would've ripped them, too.

"Yes..." I respond as I wiggle my body upwards to his raging hard erection.

"I wasn't asking, Giselle," he states matter-of-factly. He drives forward into me so hard I think my bones will actually break from the force. "I need to feel you to know that you're mine. I need to feel you to stop myself from punishing you. I need to feel you to satisfy the anger I have boiling inside of me right now." He pulls his cock out and drives forward again, this time harder as he wraps his hand around my waist, his fingers digging into my side to keep me in place.

"Punished? What...what did I do?" I ask mid-moan. He bites my neck, and I moan louder.

"You made another man want you when you belong to me, and you made me *enjoy* watching that man want you, devour you, fuck you—when I never should've shared you in the first fucking place. And now it's all I can think about. How perfect you look between us both, how perfect you fit in both of our lives."

A moment later, I hear the door click. Hogan stands there with his back against the wall as he watches us.

"I'm assuming that man is me?"

"You have terrible fucking timing. Why the fuck are you awake?" Eli groans. I look down at Eli's cock as he slides in and out of me, then look over at Hogan. "We were talking, and we think if you're ok with it, we want to see where this goes. It's not just sex anymore, I think we all can admit that." Eli pauses his movements, but remains inside me, as he speaks.

"You're ok with this? Us practically sharing you?" Hogan asks me. I bite my lip and smile at him.

"Yes. More than happy to have you boys at my feet, at my beck and call. But there's one more thing."

"Ok...what?" he asks with suspicion.

"You can't touch me yet. You can only watch and command. You tell Eli what to do to me, and he'll do it. You can touch him, if he allows you to. But I'm off limits for a little; just until we get into the groove of us as a couple adjusting into throuple."

"Mmm, I can handle that. Maybe it'll be smarter for me to move out until we figure this out?" Hogan suggests, his arms folded as he leans against the wall. He stares at Eli, running his tongue across his lip while his eyes land on his cock.

"We're not talking about that right now, but short answer? I think that's the stupidest idea you've ever said. Now, if you don't mind, I'm going to fuck our girl."

Fuck.

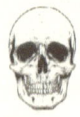

ELIAS

I roll back on top of her, pushing myself inside of her when I hear his groan and his head softly hit against the wall. I glance over my shoulder and look my best friend in his eyes, giving him the last bit of trust I have. Trust that he'll stick around.

"If you're not planning to leave, then at least sit down while you watch," I grunt. I push myself inside of Selle's pussy and she lets out a small scream. A moment later, I hear the lock on the door turn and the thud of him sitting in the chair that's in the corner of our room. I know him well enough to know that not touching her is eating him alive and knowing that gives me an odd satisfaction. Because when he is able to touch her, he's going to destroy her in the best way.

I stuff one of her breasts into my mouth and suck—hard. This is torture for her already, I know it.

"Eli, please," she begs as I slowly drag my cock in and out of her. I know what she's begging for, but she's gonna have to do better than that.

"Please what? Hmm? Please fuck you while my best friend watches? Please make you come even though you don't deserve it?" I'm teasing her, and she doesn't deserve the punishment of edging, but I can't help myself.

"Yes, please. I'm sorry. I'm yours."

"Goddamn right you are. You're his, too—just not right now." I slam into her, quickly finding my rhythm again. Her moans fill the room, and I silently thank our parents for putting us on the opposite end of the house. I flip her over, pulling her up onto her hands and knees, facing us both toward Hogan. He has his cock in his hand and he's stroking it so fucking hard I think it might break. I seat myself into Selle and she screams out again.

"Harder, Elias. Make it hurt," she moans.

"Oh, princess, you have no idea what you're asking for right now."

"You're mad, right? Show me how mad you are. Make me feel it. Please," she begs. She opens her mouth to speak again, but I wrap my hand around her neck, yanking her back to me as I fuck her relentlessly. Her eyes snap closed as the sounds of flesh against flesh echo through the room. Hogan groans as he watches—and I groan as I watch him. I can't take my goddamn eyes off him as he watches me fuck our girl, because of how angry I am at him. How angry I am at *him*, when he didn't do anything except for what I practically begged him to do. What *we* begged him to do that night: fuck my girl. That's what we told him to do, he fought us on it, told me that I wouldn't like it, and that she'd feel weird with him afterward. That it wouldn't be how it was when we fucked girls in undergrad together, because I loved this one. But I assured him that I could handle it, while Selle straight up laughed and told him not to be a pussy.

And I could—I mean I *can*—handle it. What I can't handle is how it makes me feel knowing and seeing how much he wants her; how much he wants *me*. Hogan doesn't discriminate—whatever he wants he wants, men included. I've done it a couple of times, but I've always been on the receiving end. It's never been penetrative sex, just oral. The first night with Selle and him, we crossed that line. I let him do things to me that even drunk me couldn't fathom, but I did it.

"Spank her," he commands. His voice is hoarse, but he manages to get the words out. I hesitate for a moment before bringing my hand down on her ass as my cock rushes in and out of her.

"Again. Turn her ass red." Again, I obey, this time my hand slamming down on her cheek harder.

"Good boy. Is she turning red for you?" My eyes snap to his, and Giselle tenses for a split second when my strokes slow. Did he fucking call me *good boy*? "I asked you a question, Elias. Is she turning red for you?" Selle pushes back against me and shots me a pleading look. I can't tell if it's her silently begging me to keep fucking her or if it's her begging me to ignore what the fuck just came out of Hogan's mouth. Either way, I nod to him in response and wrap my hands around her hair before fucking her harder.

"Flip her over and put her legs on your shoulders." I quickly do what he says, eager to be deeper inside of her. Her eyes are locked on me, and her pussy is on full display. I push her legs open and back up, needing to taste her before I fuck her again.

"I need to taste her first," I grunt, dropping to my knees and running my tongue through her folds. Her back arches and I splay my hand over her belly, keeping her in place. "Keep still, Giselle, or I'll make you come so fucking hard you won't be able to recover before I'm deep inside of you again. Do you understand?" She hums in agreeance, and I dig my tongue deeper inside of her.

"Does she taste good?" Hogan is now beside me, his cock still in his hand as he sits on the bed. I look at him over the hood of my eyes as I add two fingers inside of her. In an instant, my fingers are dripping with her juices. I glance at Selle, and she bites her lip, turning her attention to Hogan and his glare. His glare is not only on me, but on my soaked fingers.

"I can't touch her, I get it, but *fuck*, let me taste her." I pull her slits into my mouth and slowly lift my fingers to Hogan's mouth. He drowns himself over my fingers, sucking every drip of her off, giving a growl of satisfaction when they're licked clean. I dip them inside of her again, this time fingering her harder and deeper until she screams my name.

"Now fuck her. And when she comes..." He looks at me as my cock slowly sinks into her. "I'll be on my knees waiting to taste her."

"You know, Hogan, our girl here thinks she's incapable of getting pregnant. Should we test her theory?" I ask, feeling myself getting ready to explode.

"Mmm, make sure every fucking drop of come stays inside of her," he responds, watching my cock slam in and out of her.

I make quick work of bringing Selle to her climax. She claws my back as she soaks my cock with her juices. I'm coming harder than I thought I would, filling her with so much come that it starts leaking out of her immediately. I push it back inside of her, making her gasp as my thumb starts slowly rolling over her sensitive clit.

She pulls me to her, kissing me before moving to my ear. "Let go, like you did that night. He's going to please you, and that will please me," she whispers.

I gather my courage and turn towards him. We did say we didn't want him to touch her. When I think about it, I didn't mean it, but I'm not ready for them to know that yet. I'm still not sure if I can handle it.

"So, I can't touch her, does that mean I can't touch you, either?" he asks. I pause for a moment and take a deep breath. I shake my head, and he smirks. "Good, because as much as I want to taste her, I want to taste *you,* too."

I don't have time to respond before he's pulling my cock into his mouth.

Jesus Christ.

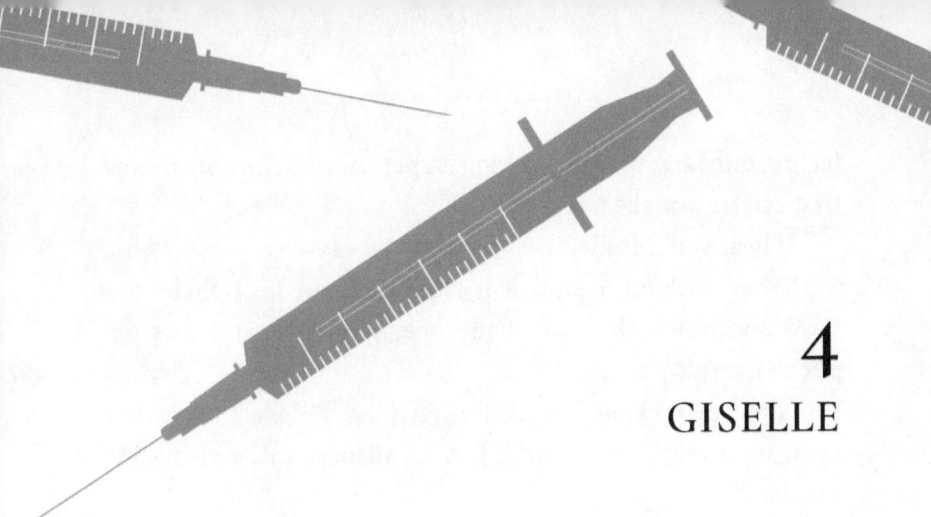

4
GISELLE

Our trip went by in a blur. Our families always get along great, and it never feels forced. But even though it was nice, I was ready to be back in my own space. Elias wasn't too happy to know that Hogan was still going to go through with his search for a place; they argued about it the entire flight home. He feels like he's losing his best friend, and Hogan feels like he's forcing our new dynamic to work by being here.

"Beer?" Hogan offers, strolling into the kitchen. We both nod and he returns with three uncapped beers in his hand. I take a sip and look between them two. Elias watches TV while Hogan scrolls on his phone. It's weird, and it's never weird.

"This is stupid. You're not moving out. It makes no sense when there is more than enough space in this apartment. And if this does continue to work, you'll be moving back in, anyway. Don't be an idiot just because you're scared."

Silence.

I look at Hogan, raising my eyebrow when he continues to scroll.

"I'm talking to you," I say. He looks up at me, noticing the frustration in my voice. I hate repeating myself, and I hate feeling unheard; they're my biggest pet peeves. The only things that can truly make me lose it.

"I hear you, Giselle."

"Then fucking acknowledge her," Eli cut in. I shake my head and down the rest of my beer while Hogan tucks his phone into his pocket.

"I'm not fucking scared. I'm terrified, Giselle," he says. I open my mouth to respond, but he silences me, putting his hand up.

"If it's this big of a deal, then I won't move out. But we're all friends first, best friends, at that. I'm not fucking that up. If I feel like I'm beginning to...I'm moving out."

"Fine, sounds good," Eli grits out through his teeth before slamming his beer down on the side table.

I tuck my feet underneath me and silently laugh at Elias' response.

This is going to be interesting.

Over the next few days, things slowly start to return to normal. The apartment is no longer filled with awkward silence, and we've all started hanging out together again. It's Thursday night, our weekly movie night, something my princess wanted to start doing when we all moved in and began working. She said it was the only way to make sure we all had uninterrupted *family time* together. She's currently laying on the couch with her head in my lap and her feet stretch out over Hogan's legs while the movie plays.

"At what point does this asshole lose his license to practice..." Selle whispers while scrolling on her phone. I peek over at her and clear my throat, but she's so deep into what she's reading, she doesn't even hear me.

"What are you talking about?" I ask, but she still doesn't pay me any attention. "Giselle." I speak up a bit louder and she snaps out of it.

"Huh? Sorry, I was doing some umm, research."

"On what?"

"Not what, but who...Remember that doctor who refused that girl her abortion to save her life?" I nod at her as she turns her phone towards me. There is a picture of the doctor, followed by pictures of various women. "Well, she's not his first victim. This asshole seems to have a reputation for either not doing the abortions or doing them and making his clients *sterile* afterward."

"Wait, what are we talking about?" Hogan asks, confused.

"There was this doctor who was basically letting women die, when an abortion could save their lives."

"How is that legal?" he asks.

"It isn't. And no one is doing anything about it. It's bullshit." She continues scrolling. "He's sponsored by someone, but I can't find the person anywhere. I'm hoping I can find him on this webpage of the founders for his clinic. Here, hand me my laptop."

She sits up, crossing her legs as I reach over and hand her the laptop. She pulls up the website and continues to look. I lean closer to her and see a link at the bottom that says *founders.*

"Click on that one, maybe it'll include photos and names." She clicks it, and sure enough, a page fills with photos of past doctors and physicians. She scrolls and scrolls, stopping on a photo that literally takes her breath and color away. She looks as pale as a ghost, and I have to nudge her to make her take her next breath. "Princess? What's wrong?"

Her eyes are full of unshed tears as she just stares that the picture. When I lean over see the photo, she slams the laptop close.

"Baby girl? What is it? Tell us," Hogan says, looking at her and then me.

"Talk to us. What happened, who is that?" I ask, rubbing her back.

"A man who shouldn't be allowed anywhere near women... I-I need to go see my brother. I'll be back later."

"Giselle, you just shut down after seeing a photo of some fucking guy. Who the fuck is he, and why did the sight of him make you look physically ill?" I ask, my voice raised a little more than I expected.

"I can't talk about it right now, Elias. I need to go, ok? I'll be back later." She slides her shoes on, grabs her keys and phone, and ignores my every move to stop her from walking out of the door.

"Giselle!" My voice is raised as she goes to open the door, only to run into Hogan first.

"Baby girl...why are you crying?" he asks as she moves to go around him. He blocks her way and pushes her further into the apartment, stabilizing himself against the door. She glares at him as her shoulders begin to shake uncontrollably, tears flowing down her cheeks.

I grab her and turn her around to face me. "Tell me what's wrong. Why are you crying about him? Is he an ex? Did he hurt you? Tell me. I can't fix it if I don't know."

Selle looks like she is going to pass out at any moment.

"He's...he's a bad man. He's a really bad man and I really need my brother right now. Please, let me go to him." I sigh and pull her into my arms, wrapping them tightly around her. I glance at Hogan, and he hangs his head, quietly stepping aside. He mouths the words *let her leave* to me and I frown, internally battling what she needs, but also keeping her safe.

"You can't drive yourself anywhere in this shape. I want you to calm down first, then I'll let you leave. Or call Graham to come get you." She nods her head and pulls out her phone, sending her brother a text to come get her. "Good girl. Go in our room until he gets here and get yourself together. I'm right here if you want to talk, ok?"

"Ok."

"Give me those lips." She smirks, wiping her face of her

tears, and gently presses her lips against mine before turning to Hogan and kissing him next. We both watch her wander into the room, finally letting out a breath when the door latches shut.

Fuck.

6

GISELLE

I'm lying against the wall; they came and hurts us again. This time, Graham took most of the hits and touching. He hasn't said much to me since the two guys left, he won't even look at me. I think he's mad at me. I'd be mad at me too. I didn't help him, all I did was scream. He always helps me and always gets it worse when he does. When I ask him why he keeps saving me, he tells it's because he's my big brother, and that's what he's supposed to do.

The door flies open, and we both jerk our heads in its direction, revealing the two men who were here an hour ago for their daily "sessions" with us. They usually will only come once a day, to give us food and water, but that soon changed. What was supposed to be them feeding us became them touching us, then it became them sticking their filthy cocks inside of us. Never mind the fact that I am twelve years old. They didn't care.

"Doctor needs to check you out, little girl." I ignore the voice I hear and close my eyes, willing them to go away. I feel hands wrap around my waist, yanking me out of the door. Graham is on his feet in a second, charging after the men. He's not quick enough, though. The door slams and I'm being yanked down the hallway before something is stuffed over my head. A moment later, I'm thrown down onto a cold surface. *Whatever was over my head is now gone and replaced with a bright light.*

"Come back in twenty minutes, she'll be ready by then." I hear a voice say before I hear footsteps retreating. I'm pulled to a sitting position before my vision is filled with the back of a tall man with a tattoo of a spider crawling up his neck. He turns around and smirks at me. "There's no way you're only twelve; you look very grown up. Giselle, isn't it?"

I nod and his smirk turns into a full smile. He runs his hands through my hair and tucks it behind my ear. "I need you to pee on this stick—have to make sure you aren't pregnant by either of those Neanderthals out there." I shake my head and force myself to speak.

"I'm not pregnant."

"And how would you know that?" I'm not about to tell him that I had my period a few days ago. That those idiots were too stupid to notice the bleeding when they were raping me. So instead, I lie.

"I haven't had a period yet." He stops briefly before tilting his head to the side, grinning.

"You're my patient, Giselle. I know everything about you. Including when you got your first period, which was exactly a year ago. Lying gets you nowhere but punished."

"I-I didn't, I'm sor—" He holds his hand up, silencing me.

"Don't apologize. Pee on this stick and then come back and stand in front of me." I sigh and grab the stick, quickly peeing on it and handing it back to him, standing exactly where he told me.

He takes a washcloth and starts gently washing each part of my body that's exposed. It's weird. And even though I know he's probably going to hit me or hurt me afterward, it's a nice change to what the other two guys do to me. The timer he set goes off. He leans over and smirks.

"Negative. Let's see if we can keep practicing while not getting you pregnant, hmm? Take your clothes off."

I step back and shake my head.

"No."

"This isn't optional. I said to take them off."

"No. Don't touch me." He smirks at me and lunges for me. I try to run, I try to fight, but I'm not strong enough. I'm never strong enough. Not even a moment later, I feel my clothes being ripped off me before he's shoving himself inside of me. He's brutal; his grip on the roots of my hair is so tight I'm beginning to get a headache.

"Please stop...stop."

"You feel so good, little girl." My stomach feels sick, but I keep fighting. "They told me you weren't a fighter. I'm glad you saved that fire for me." He slams in and out of me, and tears prick my eyes.

"I'm going to fucking kill you!" I scream.

He laughs and bites my ear.

"And I'm going to come in you."

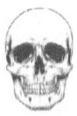

I wake up to the sound of my brother's voice as he's talking to Eli and Hogan. I sit up and shake off the dream I just had. I just need to talk to my brother, he's the only one who will understand. When I walk out of the room, Graham is standing there with his hands in his pockets. When he spots me, he raises his eyebrows.

"Ready?" he asks, and I nod. He tilts his head towards the door before he gives the guys a subtle goodbye. I kiss Eli and give Hogan a kiss on his cheek before following my brother out of the door. He stops once it shuts and looks down at me. "Selly...are you fucking them both?"

"I don't need judgment right now; I need my brother." He sighs and pulls me into his arms, giving me a tight hug.

"I'm here. Now tell me what happened." He walks me to the SUV and deposits me in it. I don't speak until we're clear of the apartment. I'm not sure why I felt like they could still hear us.

"I saw him."

"You saw who?" he asks, looking over at me and then back to the road.

"*The Doctor*..." He glares at me, and tears fill my eyes again.

"Where?"

"Online. He's a partner for this doctor who keeps killing women. He either denies them abortions when they need it, and they die, or he sterilizes them and doesn't tell them." Graham's hands tighten around the steering wheel and the car goes silent. A few moments later, we are pulling into the driveway of him and my soon- to-be sister-in-law's house.

He kills the car engine and turns to me. "What do you want to do?"

"I want to go after him. And the piece of shit doctor. And his team."

"Ok, send me the information that you found. We haven't been able to track him down for years. Are you sure it's him?"

"Graham, I'm sure. He raped me so many times, I'd know his fucked up face anywhere. And if not his face, then I'd remember that fucking neck tattoo."

He nods his head and runs his hands over his knees.

"Giselle, listen to me. Let me handle this for you. You haven't tapped into that side of the family yet. Are you sure you want to?"

"You forget that I helped you kill those two fuckers all those years ago. I haven't showed that much anger since then, because I haven't had a reason to. This is a reason. I need this. I need to do this to make a statement. Not just for me, but for all women out there: that no man can break us. That no man can make decisions for us or control our bodies without consequences. They all need to be taught a lesson. But The Doctor—he needs to die."

"Fair enough. Let me get an updated file on him and we'll plan accordingly."

"No. *I'll* plan accordingly."

"You're my baby sister. You're not going after these fuckers alone."

"G, please. I can do this."

"I'm not saying you can't, I know you can. I trained you to fight, Selly. I know you can take care of yourself, but I'll never forgive myself if something happened to you again. I'm going to be there; you do what you need to do, but I'll be there."

"Fine."

"Now, figure out when you're going to tell your boyfriend —or boyfriends—because they looked murderous when we left. And don't think you're off the hook for that shit, either. You're going to explain to me how you managed to be fucking my fiancée's brother *and* his best friend."

I shrug my shoulders and step out of the car, chuckling at him when he raises his eyebrow at me.

"Oh please, men do it all the time. Fuck society and its double standards. I like them both, who cares?"

He shakes his head, muttering *Jesus* under his breath before we walk into his house. Suddenly, I know that this revenge will give me all the power back. The power that men seem to love to take from us women.

I walk into the house and smile as my brother's fiancée pulls me into a hug.

"Hi, Selle!"

"Hi, Liza, hope you don't mind me crashing for a few hours."

"Nope, I need the girl time. Your brother is a grump

because I'm on my period." I pause and frown, because I know that Liza and I are usually on the same period schedule.

"How long have you been on?" I ask in confusion, pulling up my period app.

"Like three days? It's almost over. Aren't you on yours, too?" I play off my panic with a smirk before stuffing my phone back into my pocket.

"Of course, I am."

Fucking hell. My period is three days late.

"What do you mean it's late?" I ask into the phone at a whispering Selle on the other end. Hogan raises his eyebrow, and I shake my head, ignoring his stare.

"Exactly what I said: my period is three days late." I stand and start pacing the living room. "I'm usually on the same cycle as your sister; she's on and I'm not. I checked my app and I'm late."

"Ok, take a pregnancy test."

"I did..." she says breathless. I wait on the other end for her next words—except they never come.

"Come home. Now. Your silence can only mean one thing." She sighs and hangs up. I turn and stare at Hogan, who laughs.

"Well...I guess I'm not in the '*are you, my daddy?*' running?"

"Fuck off, Hogan."

"You're the one who could never resist coming inside of her every fucking chance you got."

"Yeah, as if you didn't want to."

"Hmm...knowing she's pregnant makes me want to do it all the more," he says, to which I swiftly punch his arm. Leave it to my best friend to make a joke out of this. I'm glad he did, though, I needed it. Because right now, I'm freaking the fuck out. And now I'm also picturing him fucking our now *pregnant* girlfriend.

"I'm sorry, man, I know this complicates things," I say.

Hogan shrugs and lays his hand on my shoulder. "If I'm allowed, I'll be there through it all, it doesn't change anything for me. But that is a decision you both have to make; so, I'll give you some space to talk with her."

TWENTY MINUTES LATER, THE BEDROOM DOOR OPENS. I WATCH THE doorframe, waiting for it to be filled with what I'm sure will be a frantic, crying Giselle. But instead, she's not crying or frantic at all; she's calm. She looks at me and shrugs her shoulders before biting her bottom lip.

"I guess I was wrong...I guess I can get pregnant..."

I hold back my smirk and instead answer in a hum.

"I guess you can. Come here."

She walks towards the bed and crawls between my legs, laying her head on my abdomen and depositing herself on her side.

"I'm sorry..." she whispers.

"Sorry for what?"

"Getting pregnant..."

"Don't apologize for something we are both old enough to know can happen. I'm not sorry."

"You're not?"

"Not the slightest. The vision of you with a swollen belly, carrying my child in there? Yeah, that's fucking hot. Hogan thinks so, too. Although I think he's jealous he didn't get to fill you with his come, and us fight over who the dad was." I chuckle.

"He knows?"

"Mhm, he heard us on the phone."

"Oh God, is he upset? He's gonna move out, isn't he?" she asks, burying her face into my stomach. I kiss her forehead and rub her back.

"Trust me, all he cared about was how fucking a pregnant lady would make his day." She tenses a bit, and I nudge her. "It's ok, princess, he's not moving out. We said we were doing this, and we're doing this—all three of us. Well, four now, I guess. But only if you're ok with it. He's willing to back out if you aren't comfortable with the idea of that."

"Wait, he still wants to do this with us?" she asks, confused.

"Mhm, he does." She smiles and then looks like she suddenly remembered something.

"Graham knows...about us three."

"What?"

"He figured it out. You two weren't so subtle with your worrying before I left, earlier. He isn't stupid."

"What'd he say?"

"He told me not to screw your friendship up. But also, to not take any shit from anyone who may make me feel bad for being happy with two men that treat me right."

"And how do you feel about that?"

"About what?"

"Being with two men who worship you and just want to love you?"

She rubs her hand over her belly and sighs.

"I don't think that would make sense to our baby, but I think we could make it our normal. I called the family doctor. He's going to come over tomorrow to draw some blood and do an ultrasound, hopefully estimating how far I possibly could be."

"I know it's a lot at once, but I'm here and I love you, ok?" I reassure her.

"I know. I love you, too, so much. And I want to tell you both about earlier, about that man, who he is, but I just need more time, ok?"

"Ok."

"I also need to go to New York, preferably before I'm all huge and pregnant, so like next week."

"Baby, I don't think you grow that fast, but ok. Just give me a date and I can come with you."

"Graham is going to come with me, it's about...the umm, family business."

"The mafia side of it?"

"...yes."

"You don't have to hide that side from me, I knew when my sister got involved with Graham that your family was danger-ous. I only suspect that you are, too, princess."

Hogan appears at the door frame and leans against it, his arms folded and a smile across his face.

"Got knocked up, huh?" he teases.

"Wanna fuck me because of it, huh?" she fires right back.

"Absofuckinglutely, but I'm not allowed to."

"You can if she tells you to. You're sticking around, right? Not running away?" I ask, looking down at Selle deposited in my arms. She starts fidgeting and I know immediately that she's getting wet thinking about it.

"As long as I'm wanted," he says, looking at us both.

She looks to him and tries to slow her erratic breathing. Her response comes out breathless, but we can make out her words.

"Then what are you waiting for? Fuck me. Both of you."

Hogan glides his tongue across his bottom lip and an evil grin spreads across my face. She has no idea what she just told us to do.

He slowly walks to the bed and drags her to the edge by her feet. He takes off her shoes one by one, followed by her socks. Her soft pink toes rest on his shoulders as he removes her leggings and panties together. I stand and round the bed, stripping out of my shirt.

"How wet do you think she is, Eli?"

"Fucking soaked. I can smell her from here," I say, yanking her shirt over her head as he sinks to his knees in front of her.

"Mmm, I wonder if she can fit us both or not," he says, flicking her pussy with his tongue, making her head fall back. I wrap my hand around her neck as he runs his tongue through her folds. When she moans, I plunge my tongue inside of her mouth and she eagerly welcomes me.

"What do you think, princess? Think that tight fucking cunt can take us both?"

"Ahh, fuck..." she moans, and I tighten my hold on her throat.

"That's not an answer, baby girl," Hogan says, looking up. He plunges his fingers inside of her and starts milking her pussy. "He asked you if you think this pretty pussy can fit both of our cocks in it. Answer him."

"...yes, yes!" she screams. I smirk at her and bite her bottom lip before whispering in her ear.

"I hope you can take it. Lay back." She leans back on the bed and watches me as I shed my pants and briefs, my cock springing in front of her face. She licks her lips eagerly. "Fuck, look at you. Greedy to suck my cock while he devours your pussy. Open up."

She opens her mouth, and I thrust my cock inside, making her gag immediately. "Mmm relax your jaw. Let me in, princess." Seconds later, I feel her force herself to swallow, and my cock slides further down her throat. Hogan takes us in over the hood of his eyes as he continuously laps up her juices.

"She tastes so goddamn good, Eli," he groans, shoving two fingers inside of her, hitting her g-spot. Her body shakes and I take this moment to brutally fuck her mouth. "Good fucking girl. You're going to come all over my mouth while Eli fills yours with his come."

Not even moments later, I'm spent, trying to hold myself up as I pump her mouth full of my come. She takes every drop, swallowing it as it hits her throat. She drinks me like it's the last thing she'll ever do, and when she's done, she comes so fucking hard Hogan has to hold her legs down from the shaking.

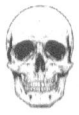

HOGAN

Goddamn. She's so fucking beautiful when she's like this. Coming all over my face. Eli can't break his stare from me, sucking the life out of her, and I know he's waiting to taste her, too.

I pull my head from between her legs and look at him with a raised eyebrow. He crawls off the bed drops to his knees next to me. His cock is still half hard, even though he just came just as hard as Selle did.

"You wanna taste her, don't you?" I question. I go to move to the side, licking my lips again, still being able to feel her juices covering my face. But he grabs me and keeps me there, and a second later, his mouth is covering mine, his tongue sucking every drop of her off mine. I wrap my hand around his cock, and he sticks his fingers inside of Selle's pussy. She screams out as he groans.

This must be heaven. I'm in fucking heaven. That's the only explanation to this.

I bite down on his lip and he groans again before pulling back and licking his lips.

"You're right, she does taste good. But I wanna feel her." The next thing I know, he's lying under her, his cock so deep inside of her that I can't fucking move from being so goddamn mesmerized. She turns to look at me over her shoulder and reaches her hand out for me. I spring into action, yanking her off him and standing her up. I bend her over, taking the back as Eli takes the front, and we both slam inside of her. Our cocks rub against each other, and I think I'll come on the fucking spot at the contact alone.

"Look at you taking us both so fucking well," Eli grunts.

"Don't lie to her, Eli, she can barely fit us both. Fuck her harder, split her open for us."

She's screaming our names, and its music to my ears. She feels like home; he feels like home. They feel...home. And I know right then are there, baby or not.

I'm never leaving.

8

GISELLE

I wake up to my phone ringing as I'm smushed between Hogan and Eli. They both have their arms around my midsection, and I feel so sweaty, but so at peace. I ignore my ringing phone until it goes off again. I slowly slide out of their embrace and grab it, sneaking into the bathroom.

"Hey, G, what's up?"

"I have the file; he'll be in New York at the end of the week." I silently calculate in my head how many days that gives me to decide what I should do. I only just found out I was pregnant. I don't know if everything is ok with the pregnancy or not, so I don't think it should get in the way of me getting my revenge. I've waited years to kill this fucker, and the fact that I get to take out the other life-sucking man with him makes it all more worth it.

Four days. Four days to plan. Four days to make sure nothing goes off without a hitch. Four days until I make a statement that women aren't fucking tools or marionettes that you can just pull the fucking strings to.

"You sure you're ok with doing this?" I ask.

"You're my sister, and that piece of shit made our lives hell. He's dying and so is his entire board. If not for us, for the women they've taken the lives and choices from." I smile into the phone, because I don't know what else I expected. My brother always has my back, no matter what.

"Ok, I'll see you soon. Love you."

"Love you, too, Selly."

I look at myself in the mirror and remind myself that I can do this. I remind myself of what he took from me. I remind myself that I'm probably not the only one he took things from. My view is crowded when it fills with Hogan wrapping his arms around me and kissing my neck.

"What are you doing up, baby girl?"

"I was going to take a bath, my body is sore," I lie.

"Hmmm, I'll run you one," he says, kissing my cheek and heading towards the tub. Taking a bath will actually help me think of my plan. I know where he is now. I know the type of business and people he's helping now. I know that he's still just as bad of a man that he was back then. The moment I drop my body into the tub, I immediately know how I'm going to get to him.

I'm going to make an appointment with one of his fellow doctors.

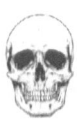

"Ok, Giselle, lie back. This will be a transvaginal ultrasound until we can figure out how far along you are."

I nod while Eli and Hogan hold my hand. The doctor who's been in our family since I was a baby inserts a probe inside of me.

"Alright...let's see here, oh! There it is, there." He turns the screen, and my heart stops when I see what he's pointing to.

"Based on the measurements on my screen, I'd say you're between eight to ten weeks pregnant."

"That's, like, almost out of the first trimester...but I had a period last month, I thought," I say in shock.

"Implantation bleeding is commonly mistaken for a period if you're not expecting pregnancy. We'll get you in for all of your testing, say, next week. In the meantime, I want you to take a prenatal and continue to live your life as you have been, but you are absolutely pregnant. Congratulations, you three," he says, glances at both Hogan and Eli. I smile at him and silently thank him for not judging as he walks out.

Eli kisses my forehead while Hogan kisses my cheek, and I laugh, because wow; I guess I'm going to be a mom. And for some reason, instead of being filled with joy, I'm filled with anger because the only thing I can think of is how many women in the world didn't get that fucking choice.

"I need to tell you both about why I freaked out...the guy I saw in the picture, he's connected to my past."

"How?" Eli asks.

"My brother and me were kidnapped when we were younger...and he's one of the men who used to hurt me. I don't want to say how, but he used to hurt me, a lot and very often. So, seeing him just reopened wounds that I basically threw salt on and kept moving without letting heal. I'm going to New York to heal them...I don't want to lie to either of you."

"Baby, we're here. Whatever you need, whatever you want to do. We're here and we'll do it," Eli says as Hogan nods.

They both kiss my cheek, and I smile, because I can do anything with the love and help of these two.

EVERY NIGHT FOR THE LAST FOUR DAYS, HOGAN AND ELI HAVE HAD ME cuddled between them while they either fuck me consecutively, or they take turns and tell each other how to fuck me. My body is sore and I'm exhausted, but I leave for New York tomorrow. The only thing fueling me is knowing that I'll be able to look at the monster who tried to take my choice away from me in the face, making good on my word and fucking kill him.

Eli and Hogan insisted on coming with me to New York. Graham told me he'd be a day late, but I just couldn't wait. Besides, it worked perfectly to me. I made an appointment for the doctor, Chance Dunridge, who refused that twenty-three-year-old an abortion. I tossed and turned all night in excitement, ready to start a literal war. Safely, of course, since ya know; pregnant and all. By morning, I was up before my alarm and ready to be in New York before we even boarded the plane.

Soon enough we were there, our car was waiting on us, and everything was going great. Eli and I made it to the doctor's office, while Hogan stayed at Graham's place he has in New York. When Dr. Dunridge's nurse calls my name and brings us back, I smirk to myself, knowing this is step one of my revenge.

"Ms. Salando, is it? Nice to meet you. My nurse tells me that you are newly pregnant and wanting top of the line care?"

"Mhm, that is correct."

"Ok, I'd be happy to help you through this journey. Is this your first pregnancy?" he asks, and I nod my head. "Do you have any concerns with this pregnancy?"

"No, I thought for quite some time that I couldn't get pregnant."

"Oh? Why's that?"

"Giselle, what am I going to do with you? You keep letting these men touch you. I know they're not smart enough to use a condom because they're greedy, I know they'd want to feel you." I'm still

looking at all of the tools he has lined up, and I'm still not scared. I'm still not fighting. "So, I'm going to make sure pregnancy isn't a problem anymore. You'll have a small little mark around your belly button, I'll go in and remove both of your fallopian tubes." My breathing increases and he lays his hand over my cheek. "Don't be afraid; it'll buy you a little time before they can touch you again. I'm doing you a favor, if you ask me."

"Just irregular periods," I lie.

"Oh, well that can happen. Since this is the first appointment, we'll get some lab work and start there. Sound good?"

"Sounds perfect."

"I'll show you where the lab room is. If your partner wants to wait here, he's more than welcome. It shouldn't take that long."

Eli nods and I follow behind Dr. Dickhead. He abruptly stops, causing me to run into the back of him.

"Oh, sorry about that. The lab is right there, I need to catch a colleague of mine before he leaves. You're in room 6; when you're all finished, you are free to go, and my nurse will call you to set your next appointment." I nod and slowly walk into the lab, telling the tech that I need to use the restroom first.

"Chance! Happy hour is in an hour, why the fuck are you still here?" I hear as I tiptoe towards the voices.

"I had a new patient come in from Seattle, told them to add her to my schedule. I just finished, why are you here? Not often the partners show up to the business they fund." Both men laugh and I take the opportunity to peek and get a glimpse. My heart starts pounding the moment I'm met with a fucking spider tattoo plastered on *The Doctor's* neck.

It's him.

I try to back up, but the nurse sees me. "Ms. Salando did you finish using the restroom?" I turn to her, but I'm too late. *The Doctor* sees me before I can hide my face. I'm not twelve anymore, but my face hasn't changed that much. He was right about one thing back then: I didn't look my age. You'd think he'd be surprised or even worried at least to see my face, but instead, he looks at me the same way he did all those years ago. *Desire.* But that's going to change, and quickly, if I have anything to do with it.

"Oh! Yes, I did," I lie. I can see him heading straight for me. I wait until he gets closer to me before I rest my hand on the door of the exit, giving him a smirk before heading through the door.

Game fucking on.

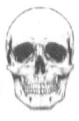

"I WISH HOGAN HAD COME WITH US TO THE APPOINTMENT. I WANT him to feel involved, you know…" I say as we walk to the car to head to Graham's place.

"I know, he said he'll be at the rest of the appointments, though. Don't worry, he's ok. I promise." We climb into the car and turn the music on. Eli puts his hand over my stomach and smirks at me. "How are you feeling?"

"Still in shock, I think, but happy I get to do this with you."

He backs the car up and my phone starts ringing, showing my brother's name. I pick it up when I suddenly see a car out of the corner of my eye. Eli slams the brakes and throws his hand over me.

"Giselle!" I hear before I hear tires screech. I don't have time to scream before the car is spinning, and somehow, we're upside down.

There's blood everywhere, and I don't know where it's coming from. Where the fuck is it coming from? I look over Selle's face and I only see small cuts. I check her neck, her arms, but there's nothing. Except when I look down, I see the blood gathering in the front of her pants.

The car hit us out of nowhere, we had barely left the parking lot of the hospital after her appointment. The appointment that she blew out of like her fucking ass was on fire. When I look up, I see people running towards us, some in scrubs and a few in white coats. I yank at her seatbelt and try to get her out, but I'm stuck, too. I pull and pull until I'm free. Something pops in my shoulder, but it doesn't matter. I have to get her out.

My door is ripped open, and someone is dragging me out, but I fight their hold. "No! Her first, get her out first! She's pregnant, and she's bleeding!" They ignore me, but a second later, her door is being tugged on.

"Her door won't open, and she won't respond. Has anyone called 911?" a man asks. His voice is calm, like this isn't something that's new to him. That makes me feel better, but not nearly enough.

"Get her out!" I yell.

"We've got her, we've got her. She's out. The doctors are going to look at her. She's a patient here, right?" I hear the lady ask me. I look up and nod, realizing it's one of the nurses. "Are you hurt anywhere?"

"No, I'm fine." I yank out of her hold and stand up, rushing behind what looks like two doctors carrying Selle into the building. "Where are they taking her?" I ask, trying to catch up with them. I stumble, but I'm determined.

"They are doctors, sir. We have an emergency labor and delivery unit. They will take care of her, I promise," she says, helping me up. When I look up, one of the doctors who has Selle turns to me and smirks. Fucking smirks. But I can't focus on that, all I can focus on is why he looks so familiar. My entire world stops when I realize where I know him from.

He's the doctor who has been killing all those pregnant women, and my fucking girlfriend is in his arms.

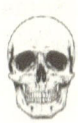

AFTER BEING FORCED TO SIT UNTIL THEY RELOCATED MY SHOULDER again, I started looking for Selle. I followed the signs to the emergency labor and delivery unit, but when I gave them her name, they told me no one by that name had been bought in.

"Check again, Giselle Salando. She was bought in probably ten minutes ago from a car accident. The fucking doctor was carrying her in here."

"I'm sorry, sir, but no doctor has been in here with anyone. Are you sure?"

I slam my hand down and take a deep breath. *Where the fuck is she?* I start to pace and pull out my phone, calling her brother.

"Salando," he answers on the other end. He's in business mode, but that's about to change.

"Graham! There was an accident, Giselle, that doctor, he took her I don't fucking—"

"Elias, take a fucking breath. I can't understand anything you're saying. What is happening?"

I gather my breath and calm myself before speaking. I'm no help if I'm frantic.

"She had an appointment today with some doctor. When we left, a car hit us. She was bleeding so fucking much, and a doctor pulled her out of the car. When I looked, it was that doctor that she showed me who was killing all of those women that needed abortions. Now I can't fucking find her. They told me they took her to the labor and delivery floor, but they checked and she's not here."

There was a brief silence before I heard a door shut.

"Elias, listen to me, closely. If that doctor took her, he's taking her to someone else. Someone who isn't just going to try to hurt her this time but kill her. Fucking find her. I'm on my way."

"Wait, what do you mean *he hurt her*?" He sighs before I hear his teeth grind.

"I don't know what Selly has told you about our childhood but...We were kidnapped and raped, constantly, every day. Selly, she had to visit someone each month to make sure she wasn't pregnant. We never knew his name, so we just called him *"The Doctor"*. He would fixate on making sure she never got pregnant but enjoyed the practice. And he *practiced* every chance he got."

"He *raped* her?" I ask, my vision turning red.

"Yeah, and then he tried to sterilize her, but it didn't work. He only got to take one of her tubes before his boss came in and stopped him. Before we escaped, she searched for him and saw him and our friend's father fleeing the building they were keeping us at. The last thing she told him was that she was going to kill him. You have to get her away from him."

"But I've never fucking seen him."

"You'll know it's him; he has a scar across his face. Selly did that."

"Ok fuck. Ok."

"You've never seen this side of our family, especially Selly, but you're about to. So, you need to figure out quickly if you can handle it or not."

"I can fucking handle it."

"Ok good, go to the apartment. In the closet there is a safe full of ammo and guns. Take them and find my fucking sister."

"I've got her." I say, hanging up and calling Hogan.

He's going to fucking flip.

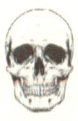

I WALK IN THE APARTMENT AND BEELINE IT FOR THE SAFE GRAHAM told me about. Hogan is on my heels, hurdling questions at me.

"What the fuck do you mean *he took her*? I don't understand this."

"You don't need to understand. All you need to know is that a prick who used to rape Giselle wants her dead and has his hands on her right now."

He stops in his tracks and watches me as I open the safe, starting to grab what I need. He doesn't say anything as I pass a gun to him, and he doesn't say anything when I grab one for myself.

I look at him and push my hands through my hair. "These doctors, they have it out for women. Pregnant women, especially for Dr. Dunridge. He waits until they need lifesaving abortions, tells them no, and lets them die—or he'll just make sure they can no longer have kids again. This other fucker, the one who she calls *The Doctor*, used to rape her and hurt her and Graham. He's the one when she wakes up, she's going to fucking do her best to kill. Our girl...she's...she's dangerous. All we need to do is find her. She'll handle the rest."

"Then let's go get our girl."

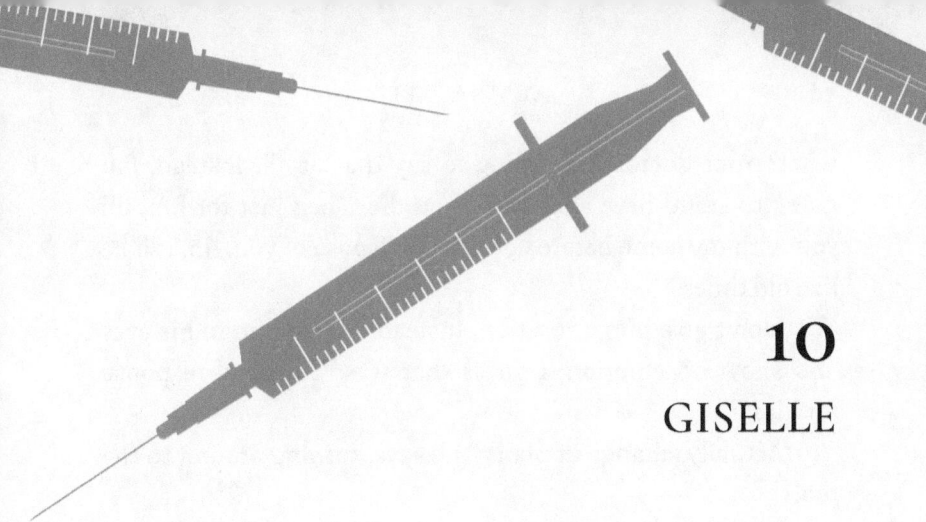

10

GISELLE

There's water dripping down my face. It's about to hit my lip, but when it does, I realize it isn't water at all. It's blood. I blink once, twice, and when I open my eyes, I feel like I'm twelve again. *The Doctor* is standing over me, with that same smile that he had all those years ago.

"Ah, there she is. I was afraid that my guy killed you with that hit. He wasn't supposed to hit on your side, but semantics." He says with a smirk.

I look down and my hand instantly flies to my stomach when I notice all of the blood on my jeans.

"Placenta abruption. The trauma from the accident separated your placenta from your uterus. So, guess what? Now you need me."

"Fuck you," I spit at him. I'll never need him. I'll never need what he does to women, what he *takes* from women. "You better kill me this time, because I promise you: in the end, it'll be *you* who needs *me*."

"The confidence is astounding. But I assure you, I'm going to deny you this abortion." He leans in close to my ear. "Because unfortunately, you aren't in a place where it's legal unless your *doctor* says it poses a threat to your life. And guess what? Your doctor isn't going to say that at all. Instead, I'm going to stand here and watch you die. Then just for fun, fill you with my come before I decide to dispose of you. Ah, it'll be like old times."

I don't give him a reaction. Instead, I stare him in his eyes and show no emotion. I guess that wasn't a good response for him.

"Actually, change of plans," he says, turning around to the tools.

He grabs the knife and slices across my stomach. It's deep, I know it is, but not deep enough to kill me. He's trying to make a statement. And when he pulls his cock out, I know that he's far from done with me. I brace myself, because I already know what comes next from this disgusting fucking man.

Sick fuck.

"Kane, the boyfriend is looking for her. He called her brother. We need to move her," Dr. Dunridge says. My skin starts crawling when I finally hear the name of the man who took so much from me. Who took so much from so many women.

"*Kane*, is it? Well, Kane, if he called Graham—you're fucked." I laugh, because I'm no longer scared. Elias and Hogan are coming, and if they've called Graham; well, let's just say that Kane will have bigger issues than me when I get out of these restraints.

The restraints that I've been working my way out of since he's been over in that corner talking with Dr. Dunridge. After we were taken, Graham made sure we knew how to get ourselves out of almost any restraint; and this one, while tight on my hands, is pretty easy to get loose enough for my hand to slip through. I twist and twist my hand until it's free from the cuff.

"So, Dunridge, what's your name?" I already know it, but I

need to buy myself time. My one hand is free, but I need to make sure they don't notice it. I'm still bleeding, and I feel weak. I don't know if I'll be able to stand once I'm free, but I'll think about that when I get to it.

"Shut up," *Kane* says. "Ignore her."

"You told me this wouldn't get out. How the fuck does she know?"

"What? That you like to have sex with your patients, patients who you've taken their choice of reproducing from? Or the fact that you like to tell them that they don't have a choice in deciding to continue or terminate their pregnancy?"

"Shut her the fuck up, Kane! She shouldn't know this!" he yells. I'm in his head, just like I hoped. He deserves it, he deserves worse. And he'll get it. Just like Kane will.

Kane waltzes over to me and draws his fist back. I brace myself for the impact and quickly shake it off. It hurts, but I don't give a fuck. Those women endured worse than what I'm getting right now. I swallow the blood that gathers in my mouth. When he turns to give Dunridge a *happy now?* look, I see the scar on his face. The one that I planted there all those years ago. I smile, knowing I'm going to do it again as my last hand slips free.

I quickly swipe the blade off the surgical table that's next to me. Dunridge sees me; his eyes go wide, but he's too slow alerting Kane. I slash it cross Kane's face, pissed off immediately because I was aiming for is throat. When he stammers back, Dunridge runs. The fucking coward actually runs. And when he pushes the door open, I realize where we are; or at least I think I know where we are.

I climb on top of Kane, the blade still in my hand. "Tell me you aren't stupid enough to be doing this shit in the same building you have thousands of people working. Unless they're all sick fucks like you?" I slash his face again, and he puts his hands up before pushing me off. I'm struggling at this point. I'm not strong enough, but if he's going to kill me, then he's going to remember me every time he looks in the mirror.

He climbs on top of me, blood dripping from the cuts on his face. "You know what? I think I'm going to save you—save you, take you, and then get you pregnant with *my child* so that you have to look at a part of me every fucking day."

He looks down at my stomach and grabs the blade out of my hand. "All I have to do is get this one out of you first." He slices the blade across my stomach, deeper this time, and I scream out. "Shh, shh, shh, I'll fix it later." He throws his head back and laughs. I lean my head back, readying myself for the instant headache I know I'll have after doing this. I drive my head forward, head butting him as hard as I can. A howl leaves his mouth, and I roll to my side, struggling to get up. This baby may not have a chance, but he doesn't get the satisfaction of killing me, too.

The moment I get to my feet, I feel a hand in my hair yanking me backward with the coldness of what I know is the blade against my neck. I close my eyes and take a deep breath, but not even a second later, the door is flying open. I can't see who it is, but all I know is it makes Kane run the opposite direction. I'm falling to the ground again, but this time, I'm caught and scooped into a pair of arms as my eyes fall on Elias.

"I've got you, princess."

"Graham! She's here, we got her!" *Hogan?*

"Fucking hell, Selly, what did he do to you? Give her to me." *Graham.* It's my brother, he came for me.

Like he always does.

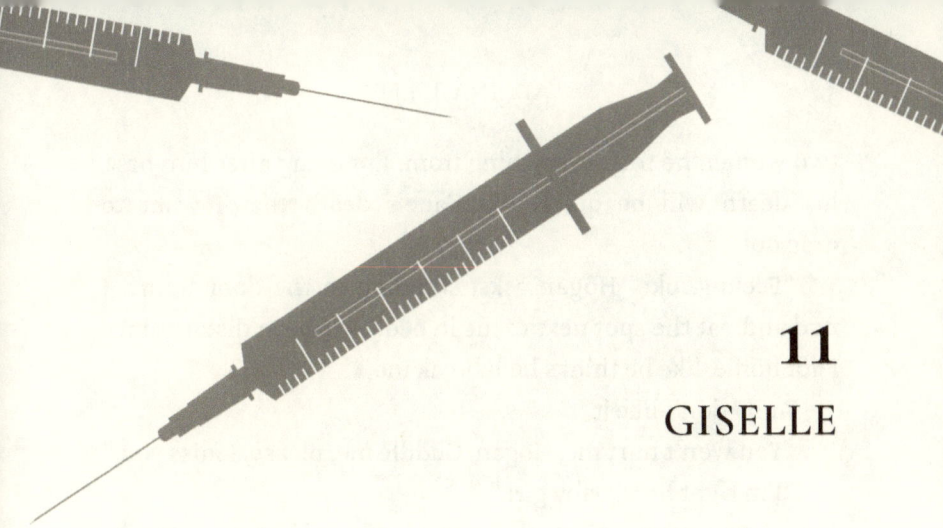

11

GISELLE

I lost the baby. It never stood a chance—it was either I die, or the baby dies. When our family doctor told us, Eli didn't hesitate to let me make the decision I wanted. He knew how important it was to me to be able to make that choice, because so many others couldn't. I wish I could say it was a hard choice, but it wasn't. The only thing going through my head when our doctor asked me what I wanted to do was Eli saying, *we can make another baby, but we can't make another you*. So, I chose to terminate. I chose it. I decided my fate, just like every woman should be able to do. No one should be able to make choices regarding my body except for me, and I'm glad Eli understood that. That doesn't change the pain of knowing who really took our baby away: *Kane*.

He and Dunridge ran off. They think that I don't know where they are, but in reality, I'm on bedrest for four weeks. Then I'm coming after them. Knowing that they'll be dead soon brings me so much joy.

I got a list of all of the woman Dunridge sterilized, and by this time tomorrow, he'll be wondering how he wired each of them $100,000 each and is now broke. I was sick to my stomach when I saw how long that list was. Fifty-two. Fifty-two women he took everything from. I'm going after him first, his death will be quick. It's Kane's death that I want to drag out.

"Feeling, ok?" Hogan asks, standing in the door frame. I nod and pat the spot next to me in bed. He's been distant since I got home, like he thinks he'll break me.

And I don't like it.

"You won't hurt me, Hogan. Cuddle me, please, I miss you."

"I'm right here, baby girl."

"Hogan, since I've gotten home, you've been treating me like the black plague. I heard you when you told me you loved me, you know...but you're not acting like it now."

He waltzes over to the bed and slides in beside me, gently pulling me onto his chest. He kisses my forehead and lets out a deep breath. Moments later, I feel wetness hitting my cheek.

"Hogan?" I ask, looking up at him.

"You almost left us. We finally decided that we didn't care what everyone else thought, that we both loved you, that we both deserved you, and then you almost died. We wouldn't have gotten the chance to love you. We wouldn't have gotten the fucking chance to show you how much we could deserve you."

"Hogan, I'm right here, and I didn't go anywhere. I'm sorry, ok? I'm sorry, I didn't mean to get hurt. I should've told you both about what happened to my brother and I, but I didn't know how to. I didn't know how to tell you that I was raped so many times that I lost count. I didn't want either of you to think differently of me..."

"Why would we think any of those things? If anything, we'd think about how strong you are. And how you fought back? Crazy. Definitely crazy."

I chuckle, and he squeezes me and laughs himself. It's the first time I've heard him laugh since I've been saved.

I sit up and he rubs my back. "I happen to love you, too, you know? And the only person's opinion I cared about already knows, and he doesn't care. He just wants me happy."

"I know, he talked to me. Told me the same thing he told Eli: I hurt you, he kills me."

"Yup, that's my brother."

"He also told us that the Giselle we're going to see is a different person. A dangerous person."

"Yeah, well, don't worry. I can shut her off pretty quickly. I just need to get my revenge first."

"A good girl and a bad one all in one? I really am fucked."

I sit up on my knees and lean in, planting a gentle kiss on his lips before giggling. "Yeah, you are, but I love you. Wanna show me just how fucked you are, though?"

He sighs, tucking a strand of my hair behind my ear. "I love you, too, but no."

"Why not? Sex is fine, I'm not bleeding anymore. Gonna make me beg? Where's Eli? He won't tell me no," I say, looking behind me to the door.

"Picking up some food, he'll be home soon. But the answer is still no." His eyes gaze over to the healing knife wound Kane left on my stomach.

"Come on, neither of you have touched me in almost a month. I need to feel you; I need to feel him. I need to be touched. Please, I'm fine."

"Giselle...I don't want to hurt you. We just want to love you right now."

"Then do it slowly," I say. He kisses my forehead and lets out a sigh of defeat. I perk up, knowing I'm winning.

"Extremely slow. Can't hurt my girl."

"Hmm not used to you being the nice one."

"Mhm, I know," he says, lifting my shirt over my head

when the door opens. "There he is." He says kissing me gently on my shoulder blade.

Eli fills the doorframe and smiles when he sees us.

"Gonna join us?" I ask. He smirks at me as he walks towards the bed.

Hogan kisses my neck, making me moan, while Eli attacks my mouth. It's gentle but rough at the same time, full of hunger, and my body comes alive. Hogan works his lips down my body while Eli glides down next to him, removing my shorts and panties. He runs his tongue across my pussy folds, and my back arches. Hogan's fingers join Eli's tongue, and I feel like I'll come immediately from the pressure of both. Eli is twirling his tongue around in circles while Hogan slowly pushing his fingers in and out of me. I'm moaning louder and louder at this point. My body grows hungry for both of their cocks; it's what I need. I need to feel them, together.

"Fuck me, please," I groan. They give each other a look and I know they're contemplating denying me. "Please..."

"Slow and gentle, Giselle. Do you understand?" Hogan says, and I nod.

"No, tell us you understand," he continues. Eli tilts his head and raises his eyebrow at me as he waits, looking up at me from between my legs.

"I understand."

Not even a second later, I'm being filled by both of their cocks. It's like my pussy has gotten accustomed to fitting both of them. We all groan in unison; taking a second to just feel each other.

"Fuck, I missed this," Eli says as he pushes in and out of me. "It's been four weeks, and you can still fit us like you belong to us."

"She does belong to us. Don't you?" Hogan asks as he pushes deeper into me, running his tongue over my neck.

"Yes. Yes...No one else," I say as they pull out of me. Eli gets behind me and Hogan stands in front of me, I'm now face to face with his bulging cock. Eli slams into me and I grab onto Hogan to keep myself from falling over. He taps his cock against my lips.

"Open up and swallow my cock, baby girl." I quickly oblige, and he fucks my mouth, brutally. There's nothing slow or gentle about it, but I can tell from the way he's looking at me that he knows it's not even close to what I need right now. I need to feel him gripping my hair tightly from the roots. I need to feel the burn of vomit threatening to come up from my throat because he is so deep. I need to feel all of him. "You are a goddamn vision, taking both of our cocks so well."

Eli's hand slaps across my ass and I moan around Hogan's cock. I'm going to come. I can't last, and I hope they're with me.

"She's going to come. Her pussy is so tight around me, she's practically squeezing me into coming with her. Get there, Hogan, because I'm fucking done," he grunts as I start to viciously come. Eli fucks me through my orgasm, and a minute later; my mouth is full of Hogan's saltiness. I swallow every drop of him as Eli fills my pussy with his come.

We all collapse onto the bed. Eli kisses my forehead, bringing my attention to him.

"Hi, baby," I say. Tears fill his eyes, and he runs his hand down my cheek.

"Hi, princess. Don't ever scare us like that again, ok?"

"Can I make that promise in four days?"

They let out a collective sigh before Hogan groans.

"Fucking Salandos."

12

GISELLE

It's game time. I feel good, and I'm ready to get revenge for not only me, but all of those other women. We're going after Dunridge first, he's at his private practice in Oregon. I'm sure he thought I wouldn't find him there, but we did. And it wasn't hard to, either.

When I told Eli and Hogan what I was planning to do, they both said they were coming without hesitating. My brother came, too, of course. He had to tell Liz what was going on so that she wouldn't worry. I wasn't happy that my new sister-in-law would know my dark, disgusting past, but when she texted, me saying she loved me and to give them hell, it made me love her even more.

"Quick and easy, Selly. No mess. Not this time," Graham says, passing me a gun and a silencer. I pout and he raises his eyebrow at me. "It's bad enough that I'm letting you do this in the middle of the fucking day. You heard me— quick and easy."

"Fine," I say, shoving the gun into the back of my waistband. When we pull behind Dunridge's office, I grab my black leather jacket and throw it on. Eli and Hogan slide out behind me, but Eli grabs my arm when I turn for the back door of the building.

"Be smart, Giselle."

"Ooo, *Giselle*, huh? I must be in trouble if you're calling me that."

"Hey, no fucking around. I'm serious. Be fucking smart."

"Ok, ok, I will. Relax, cowboy, you'll be right there if I become, I don't know, *reckless*." I chuckle, and he pushes his hand through his hair as I slowly open the back door. Graham goes first, and I follow behind with Eli and Hogan close.

"Ellis, who's in this building right now?" Graham asks in his earpiece, to the man who has been in our family protecting us since we were kids.

"It should just be him, but I'm picking up another thermal body heat in his office. On your right, two doors down."

Graham turns around and signals me to be quiet. I raise my eyebrow and nod. He nods his head towards the door that's Dunridge's office. He looks at me and I take a deep breath.

"Ready?" he whispers. I nod my head, and he smirks. "Give em' hell, Selly." With that, he kicks the door in. I waltz in, stopping in my tracks when I see an unconscious woman lying on his desk.

"Couldn't go longer than a month, huh? Sick fuck." He practically jumps off her and stuffs his dick back into his scrub pants. I pick up her folder on the desk and read over it. The patient came in for an abortion. I look at her date of birth and flinch. She's seventeen-years-old, she most likely wasn't ready to be a mom. "Guys, can you get her out of here, make sure she's, ok? I'm not sure what he did to her."

"I'm not leaving you," Eli says. Graham looks from me to him, and I nod in agreeance.

"Fuck being quick and easy—destroy this son of a bitch," Graham grits out as he helps the girl out of the room.

"Got it." I turn back to Dunridge who has practically backed himself into a corner. Hogan locks the door as Eli leans against it. I stalk closer to Dunridge. "Do you remember her name?" I ask him. He swallows hard as I take the gun from my waistband and start screwing the silencer on it. "Do you remember her name? Please don't make me ask again."

"Yes...Yes, it's Anna." I shake my head. Fucking bastard.

"Nope, it's Amber. I sure hope you at least remember what she looked like, because she's the last victim in your pathetic little life."

"Look, I'm sorry—"

"I don't care how fucking sorry you are. Be sorry to the women you took rights from. Be sorry to their futures you stole. She was fucking seventeen-years-old, and you raped her. She came to you for a fucking abortion because that's her goddamn right, and instead you drugged her and raped her!"

"You don't understa—"

"I'm tired of hearing your voice," I say putting my hand up. I raise the gun and shoot one kneecap, before quickly taking out the other, making him scream in pain. "You never did get to have your way with me, did you?" His eyes narrow at me, his breathing accelerated. "What's wrong? Not used to not getting what you want from women? Was that your deal with Kane? You helped if you got to get your dick wet?"

His pain turns to rage. "He promised you to me. He promised that I would get a chance at that pussy he always talked about," he grinds out.

I turn to Eli and raise my eyebrow. He's leaned against the wall with his hands in his pocket. "What do you say, babe? Want to show him what he is missing out on?" He smirks and walks over to me before I stand and yank my pants down. Not a moment later, he pulls his cock out.

"I tell you what, we'll show you what it should look like to fuck someone who wants to be fucked, who wants to be filled with come. I'll even give you an opportunity for one last chance to come before I kill you myself."

"Are you wet?" Eli whispers in my ear. I nod, biting my lip.

"Mhm. Find out," I tease. He chuckles and pushes his fingers into my pussy, my pussy that instantly became wet the moment he leaned off that damn wall. "Fucking perfect like always. It's been a while since I've had you to myself, but this will be fast and hard. Like you said, we're on a tight schedule. Legs open."

I quickly oblige and he sinks inside of me, causing me to scream out. And just like he said he would, he fucks me hard and fast. I hear Dunridge grunt as he starts jerking himself off, hate and jealously swimming in his eyes as he watches us. I can barely keep up with Eli's thrust and I don't try to. I let him take charge as he yanks my head back. He pushes deeper into me, causing me to cry out. "Come for me, Giselle. I told you quick and I meant it." I squeeze my pussy around him and groan into his next thrust. "Now I'm going to fill you with my come. We both know it's your favorite thing for me to do. Isn't it?"

"Yes, fuck yes. Do it." I feel the warmth shoot through me and I scream out Eli's name.

When he's finished, he shields me with his body as I pull my pants back on. When I turn my attention back to Dunridge, he is covered in his own come. There's blood around him, pouring out of his knees, and he's drenched in sweat. Hogan holds him back as I take a knife, cutting his scrubs off his body. I grab a syringe and fill it with his come, then attach a needle on the end of it.

"Don't move too much, it'll hurt a lot worse if you do," I warn as I stick the tip of the needle in his cock. He screams out in pain, and I smile as I push his semen back inside of him.

"See, you don't like it, do you? I don't think they did, either. You piece of fucking shit."

I push him onto the ground, pulling out a knife from my jacket. I look to Eli and Hogan, raising my eyebrow. "I'm going to cut his dick off, maybe turn away?"

"Nope, we wanna watch our girl work," Eli says, leaning against the chair as he watches. I shrug before picking up Dunridge's dick, slicing the knife through it as he screams out in pain. "I plan on doing this to your friend Kane, too. Both of you will die similar deaths, although his will be a lot more painful. Open your mouth." He shakes his head, and Hogan grabs his face, squeezing it just enough to where I can shove his cock in his mouth. I take the knife and run it across his throat. "Have fun in hell."

Looking up and facing my men, I expect them to look shocked, disgusted, or even scared. But they don't. They are fucking smiling at me.

"That's our girl," Hogan says. I kiss both of them, look over my shoulder at the blood pooling out of Dunridge, and walk out of the door.

KANE WAS ONLY ABOUT AN HOUR AWAY. APPARENTLY, THEY ALL DO their dirty work together, with close locations. His house was tucked away in the woods—you wouldn't know anything was back there if you didn't check. Which is what makes him think he's safe. But he's not. He's mine. Finally.

"Do I have to be quick and quiet with this one, too?" I ask Graham as we all climb out of the car. He smirks at me and pulls out a knife, handing it to me.

"Do your worst, Selly."

I snag the knife from him and kiss his cheek, practically skipping to the front door. I don't bother sneaking in, it won't matter. It's five of us, if I include Ellis, and only one of him. So, I walk right up to the front fucking door and jiggle the handle. It's locked, but not for long. Hogan slides me out of the way, aims his gun, and shoots the lock right off.

"Thanks, baby," I say to him as he smirks back. When I walk in, I glance around, but the house is silent.

"*Honeyyyy, I'm home*! Aren't you gonna come greet me?" I hear footsteps above me, and I look up to see his shadow next to a window. "Aww, don't be shy, I just wanna talk."

"How'd you find me?" he asks, malice dripping from his voice.

"Kane, that's not important. What is important is that I'm here now. Don't be rude to your guests."

"*Guests?*" he asks as I watch him load a gun, walking down the steps. I know he's buying time; but so am I. Graham is inching his way around the stairwell, and he has no idea.

"Yes. And I believe one is right behind you," I say when he raises the gun towards me. He shoots, and Eli all but tackles me to the ground. When he turns around, Graham smiles at him.

"Kane, is it? All these years and we never knew your name. I can't wait to let my sister kill you." He takes his gun and rams it into Kane's face, blood spurting everywhere. Then he takes his fist and right hooks him.

Yup, he's knocked out. The guys move him and tie him to a chair. I take my knife and run it across his chest, making him scream out in pain.

"Ahh, look at that—you do feel pain, after all. I can't wait to add to those scars I gave you all those years ago. But first, I'm going to line each of these perfect tools up, just like you did."

"Giselle, come on. We can talk," he begs.

"What is it with you and Dunridge wanting to talk? There's nothing to talk about." I lean down in his face, and whisper to him, "But we are going to record you admitting everything you've been doing to all these women. Then we're going to send it to the board of your company. It won't matter really, because you'll be dead, but it sure will make me happy."

I pick up the phone and aim it at him. "You're going to admit to exactly what you have been doing, how you've been abusing your power. How you've been stripping women from their basic human fucking rights. And if you don't, I'll just kill and expose you, anyway."

"Ok, ok, stop, please. I'll do it. I'll do it." I laugh to myself because he didn't have a choice.

I pick the phone back up and nod at him when the video starts. He starts spilling everything, from the time he raped me to the time he started denying women abortions since it was legal in some states. He explained how him and his coworker would sterilize them and then have sex with them. Then he ended it with how to get the files with all of the victims' names on it.

I end the video and tilt my head at him. "Wow, that was great. I mean seriously, what a good sport!" The guys try to hold back their laughs behind me, but I shrug it off. I take the knife my brother gave me, picking up one of Kane's fingers before slicing through it. "But too bad, I had already made my choice to kill you."

He screams again as I take the knife and slice through another finger. I push his hand to the side and watch as he starts to bleed everywhere.

I walk around him and look to Graham. "Want in on this?" He pauses for a second and Hogan growls.

"If he doesn't, I do," he says.

"Me too," Eli jumps in. I laugh and throw the knife at Hogan. He catches it with swiftness and quickly takes the knife to Kane's face, slashing twice. Eli circles him as Hogan finishes up and passes him the knife. Kane is covered in blood, and it brings me a slither of happiness. Eli bends down and grabs his ear. "You'll never touch her or anyone else again." He takes the knife and slices across his stomach.

"I have an idea...didn't he use things on you, Selly?" Graham asks. I nod, and he grits his teeth. He eyes the table I organized with random objects around the house. He grabs a candlestick. "Stand him up, pull his pants down."

"Oh wait!" I say, grabbing the knife from Eli. I grab Kane's cock and slowly drive the knife through it. His screams fill the house, and my insides are on fire. "That's for taking one of my fallopian tubes, you sick fuck." I take his balls and slice the knife through each of those next. Then I take his dismembered cock and balls, shoving them in his mouth before pushing his face back into the chair. "And this is for taking advantage of me as a fucking child." I look at my brother and he shoves the candlestick up Kane's ass. I walk over and grab the stick, pushing it in and out of his ass as he screams. "It doesn't fucking feel good when you're forced to do something, does it?" I let go and Graham pulls out a lighter, looking to me.

I take a step back and take in the scene. My old rapist, being destroyed by three men who would shake the fucking world for me. I'm happy, but I still sigh.

"I expected this to feel good. But I'd feel better if it were some of those women getting their revenge, too," I say, turning to my brother.

"Selly, we will get the list and take care of them. They'll never want for anything. Kill him and let's go. I have a fiancée to get home to and you have a life to start. A life without looking back and having to remember this piece of shit."

I look at Hogan and Eli and realize how right he is. I can't let him have any more power over me, over those women that I'm sure are looking over their shoulders every day.

I walk behind him, yank his head back, and slit his throat. I smile as blood sprays everywhere from severing his artery. Then I round his body as he grasps his neck, trying to stop the bleeding. I laugh as I jam the knife into the bottom of his stomach and yank it upward. A moment later, his insides start falling at my feet before his body slumps over.

"Told you I'd kill you. I hope hell treats you shitty. And if you were wondering, you and your shitface of a doctor friend died the exact same way, except you got fed your dick *and* balls," I say, releasing his head and nodding at Graham. He downs him in gasoline that we brought before throwing the lighter, his body now engulfed in flames.

I stand there with my arms folded watching as the childhood trauma, the bad decisions in men, the feeling like I had no control over my life, and future go up in flames in front of me. I feel empty, but yet so full. I feel...happy.

"That was fucking hot," Hogan says to Eli. I hear Graham groan, and I laugh. "Do we have time for a quickie?"

"Oh, for fuck's sake! I'll be outside," Graham says, barging out of the door. I giggle and pull Hogan in, shoving my hand down his pants the moment my brother disappears.

"You wanna fuck me while my rapist is being burned alive behind us?" I ask, biting his lip. He nods and lifts me, pushing me against the door.

"Goddamn right, I do. Eli?" He smirks and sits in the chair next to the door.

"I'll watch this time. She's all yours." Hogan smirks while pulling our pants down. He lifts me, gliding me onto his painfully hard cock. I scream out as he shows no mercy on me, pushing in and out of me each time harder than the first.

I do my signature move and tighten my pussy around him. And when I repeat the motion, I know by his reaction he's going to lose it.

"Fuck!" he screams out.

"Don't tell me both of my boys are quick today?" I tease, doing it again. He pushes his hands through my hair and yanks, exposing my neck before he bites down on it. He pumps in and out of me, and I relish in the feeling of his hands in my hair.

"Get there, Giselle. Your brother is outside, and this house is filling with smoke."

"Then fuck me harder and do what Eli did earlier. Fill me with your come. All of it, give it to me," I say, he does and then I'm coming so hard I think I'll faint with him following right behind me, filling me with his come.

"Ahh fuck...so fucking good, baby girl," he groans in my ear as he comes. He kisses my forehead and sets me down on my feet, placing my pants back in place.

I look at Eli, and he smirks as I walk over to him. He plants a kiss on my lips, and I melt all over again.

"I love you both. So much," I say, looking between them both.

"We know. And we love you, too. Now let's get the fuck out of here," Eli says.

Everything will be fine.

GISELLE'S NOTE TO READERS

If you are a woman who is currently pregnant, and you feel that for whatever reason you aren't ready, or if you have a life-threatening medical reason and need to terminate your pregnancy, that is your fucking right. Don't let anyone, especially a man, tell you otherwise. Advocate for yourself. Fight for yourself, for the other women out there who didn't get that choice. Always know that you are the only person who can make a difference in your life. You want to be a mom? Great. You don't want it to be right now, at this time in your life? Great. You want to freeze your eggs? Great. You want to try IVF to get pregnant? Great. Do whatever YOU want to do and tell society and the government to kiss your fucking ass.

But after all, maybe don't listen to me—I'm the one screwing two best friends. Society probably thinks I'm a slut, and guess what? They can kiss my fucking ass.

ACKNOWLEDGMENTS

It's always so surreal when I finish another book. When I write that last word, the imposter syndrome sits in and I stare at it for bit before I realize, holy shit I did it. My readers, you've been with me from the beginning, you've seen the growth and given me the determination I need to keep writing; so first I want to thank YOU! Secondly, Hannah, my editor that made this feel worthy of being written. You always know exactly what I'm trying say without making me change my voice. I absolutely adore you. Shay, this interior is breathtaking, and you didn't think twice about adding me to your INSANELY busy schedule. Thank you for always being flexible with me. Anna, you sweet girl! This cover is beautiful, and all I had to do was give you vibes and you did the rest. Kala and Olivia, thank you for letting me bounce ideas off you both.

ALSO BY ALAINA T. LEE

If you enjoyed this book, please look below to continue your reading journey with me. It will always be spicy, dark, emotional, sexy and full of good banter. Your FMC will always be strong and independent and your MMC will always be dark and moody, but a pocket of sunshine for our girl. Other releases are listed below. Happy reading!

Xoxo,

Alaina

Tantalized and Insatiable: book 1 and 2 in the "Angel" Series

Ruins: book 1 in the "Redcrest University" Series

All are available on KU and Amazon.

www.ingramcontent.com/pod-product-compliance
Lightning Source LLC
Chambersburg PA
CBHW020649250626
47154CB00008B/2877